D0549705

DC SUPER FRIENDS™
FLYING HIGH

FLYING HIGH
A BANTAM BOOK 978 0 857 51126 3

Published in Great Britain by Bantam, an imprint of Random House Children's Books
A Random House Group Company.

This edition published 2012

1 3 5 7 9 10 8 6 4 2

RHUK26798

The Random House Group Limited supports The Forest Stewardship Council® (FSC®), the leading international forest certification organisation. Our books carrying the FSC label are printed on FSC® certified paper. FSC is the only forest certification scheme endorsed by the leading environmental organisations, including Greenpeace. Our paper procurement policy can be found at
www.randomhouse.co.uk/environment

Bantam Books are published by Random House Children's Books,
61–63 Uxbridge Road, London W5 5SA

www.**kids**at**randomhouse**.co.uk www.**totallyrandombooks**.co.uk www.**randomhouse**.co.uk

Addresses for companies within The Random House Group Limited can be found at:
www.randomhouse.co.uk/offices.htm

THE RANDOM HOUSE GROUP Limited Reg. No. 954009

A CIP catalogue record for this book is available from the British Library

Printed in China

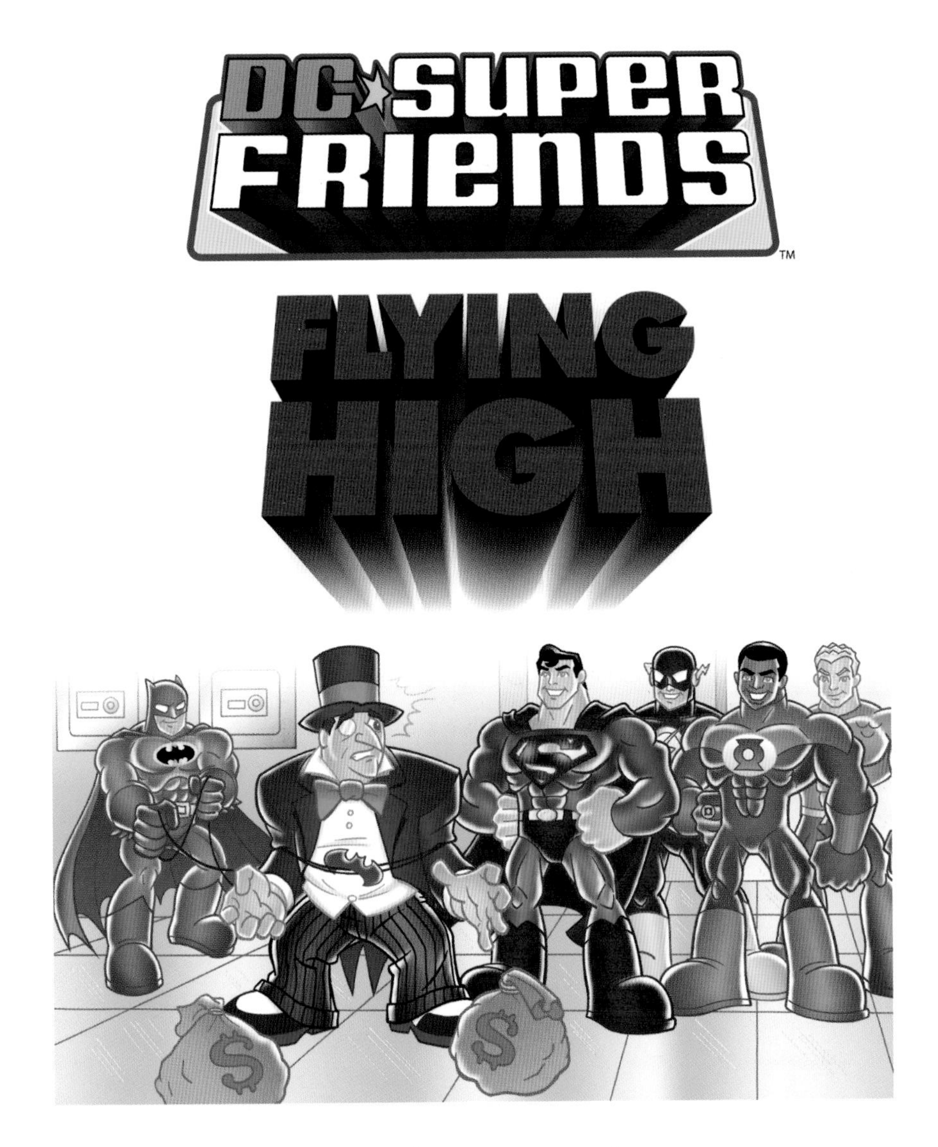

by Nick Eliopulos

illustrated by Loston Wallace and David Tanguay

BANTAM BOOKS

Batman swings
over Gotham City.
The sun is shining.

But something
strange is in the air.
The Super Friends
have work to do.

Honk! Honk!

Pigeons block traffic.

CITY BUS

The Flash races

to the rescue!

The pigeons
fly away.

Caw! Caw!

At the beach,

seagulls steal food.

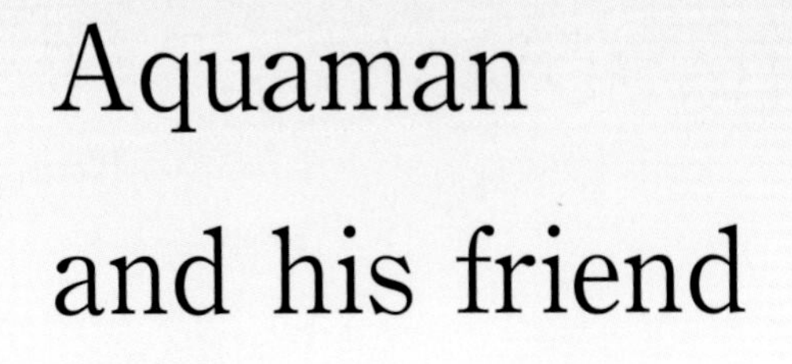

Aquaman
and his friend

make a big splash!

Squawk!

Ostriches run away from the zoo.

Superman and
Green Lantern
fly to the rescue!

They stop the birds
in their tracks.

Hmmm.

Batman spots a clue.

It is a strange machine.

Batman takes
a closer look.
The noisy machine
bothers the birds.

ON
OFF

Now the birds
are happy again.

Inside, the Penguin

robs the bank.

"The Super Friends
are too busy!
They can't stop me,"
he says.

But Batman leaps into action.

He stops the Penguin's evil plan.

Teamwork saves the day!

EXIT